Anonymous

A Book of Nursery Rhymes

Anonymous

A Book of Nursery Rhymes

ISBN/EAN: 9783337259822

Printed in Europe, USA, Canada, Australia, Japan

Cover: Foto ©Andreas Hilbeck / pixelio.de

More available books at **www.hansebooks.com**

A BOOK·OF NURSERY·RHYMES

ILLUSTRATED·BY·FRANK·D·BEDFORD
PUBLISHED·BY
DOUBLEDAY·McCLURE·Co.
NEW·YORK
1897

CONTENTS

THE·WHALE·

The whale, the whale, and now must we sing
The ocean's pride and the fishes' king.
He is the vast and the mighty thing,
    Sailing along in the deep blue sea.

Down to the bottom sometimes he goes,
Then up to the surface again for blows,
And when he has done then off goes he,
    Sailing along in the deep blue sea.

In Northern climes where it is very cold,
This fish is found, as I've been told,
And there will sport in his mighty glee,
    Sailing along in the deep blue sea.

'Tis a dangerous thing in catching the whale,
He'll toss o'er the boat with a flick of his tail,
And when he's done so, off goes he,
    Sailing along in the deep blue sea.

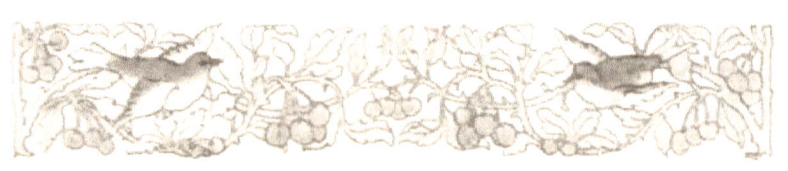

GOOSEY·GOOSE·GANDER

GOOSEY GOOSEY GANDER
WITH HER GOSLINGS UNDER

TOM·THUMB·

Tom Thumb, the Piper's son,
Stole a pig and away did run.
The pig was eat, and Tom was beat,
Till he ran crying down the street.

DANCE·A·BABY·DIDDY·

Dance a baby diddy ;
What can Mammy do wid'e ?
Sit in a lap, give it some pap,
And dance a baby diddy.

Smile, my baby bonny ;
What will time bring on'e ?
Sorrow and care, frowns and grey hair ;
So smile, my baby bonny.

Laugh, my baby beauty ;
What will time do to ye ?
Furrow your cheek, wrinkle your neck ;
So laugh, my baby beauty.

Dance my baby deary,
Mother will never be weary,
Frolic and play, now while you may ;
So dance, my baby, deary.

DANCE·A·BABY·DIDDY·WHAT·
CAN·MAMMY·DO·WID'E·

MY·JOHNNIE

My Johnny was a shoemaker,
  And dearly he loved me;
My Johnny was a shoemaker,
  But now he's gone to sea.
With nasty pitch to soil his hands,
  And sail the stormy sea;
    My Johnny was a shoemaker.

His jacket was deep sky blue,
  And curly was his hair;
His jacket was deep sky blue,
  It was as I declare.
To reef the topsail now he's gone,
  And sail across the stormy sea,
    My Johnny was a shoemaker.

And he will be a captain, by and by,
  With a brave and gallant crew;
And he will be a captain, by and by,
  With a sword and a spyglass too.
And when he is a captain bold
  He'll come back to marry me;
    My Johnny was a shoemaker.

SIMPLE·SIMON·

Simple Simon met a pieman
   Going to the fair ;
Says Simple Simon to the pieman,
   ' Let me taste your ware.'

Says the pieman to Simple Simon,
   ' Show me first your penny.'
Says Simple Simon to the pieman,
   ' Indeed I have not any.'

Simple Simon went a-fishing
   For to catch a whale ;
All the water he had got
   Was in his mother's pail.

Simple Simon went to look
   If plums grew on a thistle ;
He pricked his fingers very much,
   Which made poor Simon whistle.

SIMPLE · SIMON · MET · A · PIE -
-MAN · GOING · TO · THE · FAIR ·

WEE·WILLIE·WINKIE·

Wee Willie Winkie runs through the town,
Upstairs and downstairs in his night gown,
Tapping at the window, crying at the lock,
'Are the babes in their beds, for it's now ten
    o'clock?'

CURLY·LOCKS

Curly locks! curly locks! wilt thou be mine?
Thou shalt not wash dishes nor yet feed the
      swine ;
But sit on a cushion, and sew a fine seam,
And feast upon strawberries, sugar, and cream.

CURLY·LOCKS, CURLY·LOCKS,
WILT·THOU·BE·MINE

GEORGIE-PORGIE

Georgie Porgie pudding and pie,
Kissed the girls and made them cry;
When the girls came out to play,
George Porgie ran away.

NEW·YEARS·DAY

I saw three ships come sailing by,
   Come sailing by, come sailing by;
I saw three ships come sailing by,
   On New-Year's day in the morning.

And what do you think was in them then,
   Was in them then, was in them then?
And what do you think was in them then,
   On New-Year's day in the morning?

Three pretty girls were in them then,
   Were in them then, were in them then.
Three pretty girls were in them then,
   On New-Year's day in the morning.

One could whistle, and one could sing,
   The other could play on the violin,
Such joy there was at my wedding,
   On New-Year's day in the morning.

I·SAW·THREE·SHIPS·COME·
SAILING·BY·COME·SAILING·
BY

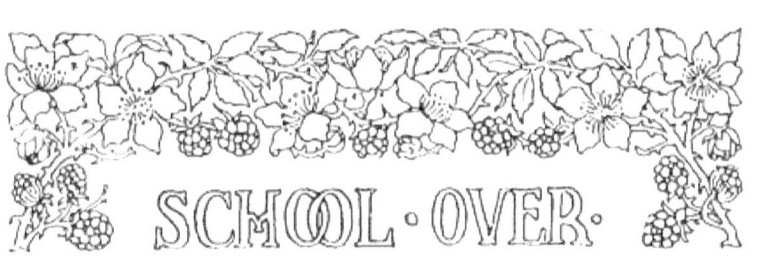

SCHOOL·OVER·

When our working school is done,
    To the fields we go,
Walking in the grassy paths
    Skipping we go.
Picking cooling buttercups,
    Many pretty flowers,
Violets, forget-me-nots,
    Spend happy hours.
Chase the bee and butterfly,
Where the summer daisies lie.

Ofttimes up the hills we go,
    Gather pretty flowers,
Bluebells and daffodils,
    Spending happy hours.
See little streamlets dance,
    Down the hill side,
See the rocks the sunbeams glance,
    Whence they glide.
Chase the bee and butterfly
Where the summer daisies lie.

LITTLE·MISS·MUFFET·

Little Miss Muffet
Sat on a tuffet.
Eating of curds and whey:
There came a little spider,
Who sat down beside her,
And frightened Miss Muffet away.

LITTLE · MISS · MUFFET · SAT ·
ON · A · TUFFET · EATING · OF ·
CURDS · AND · WHEY ·

BAH·BAH·BLACK·SHEEP.

Bah! bah! Black Sheep,
  Have you any wool?
Yes, marry, have I
  Three bags full.
There's one for my master,
  And one for my dame,
But none for the naughty boy
  Who cries in the lane.

GIRLS & BOYS COME·OUT·TO·PLAY

Girls and boys come out to play,
The moon doth shine as bright as day ;
Leave your supper and leave your sleep,
And come to your playfellows in the street.
 Come with a whoop, and come with a call.
 Come with a good will or not at all.
 Up the ladder and down the wall,
 A penny loaf it will serve us all.
 You find milk, and I'll find flour,
 And we'll have a pudding in half an hour.

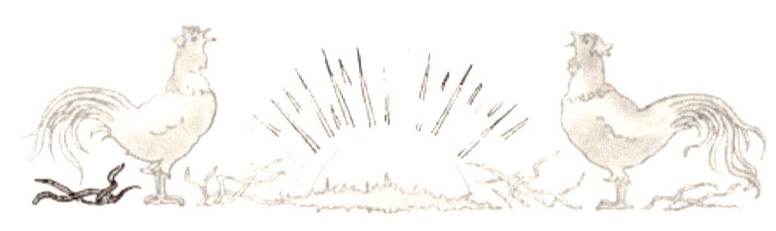

GIRLS·AND·BOYS·COME·
·OUT·TO·PLAY·

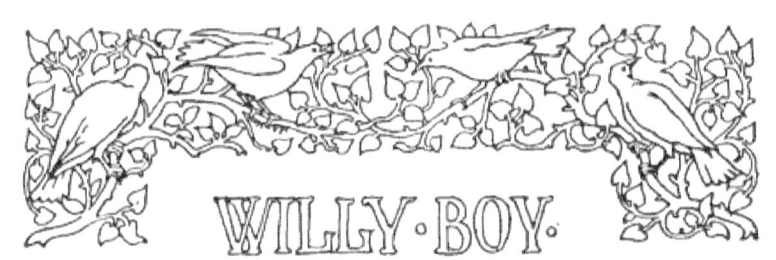

WILLY·BOY·

' Willy boy, Willy boy, where are you going?
   I will go with you, if I may.'
' I am going to the meadows, to see them mowing,
   I am going to see them make the hay.'

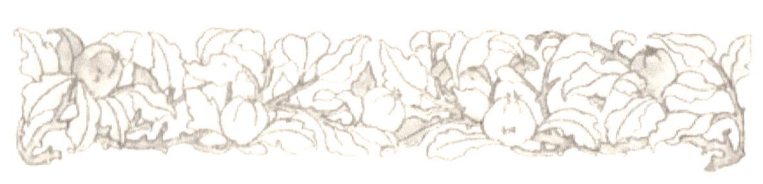

LITTLE·BOY·BLUE·

Little boy Blue, blow your horn,
The cow's in the meadow, the sheep in the corn.
But where is the little boy tending the sheep?
He's under the hayrick fast asleep.

LITTLE·BOY·BLUE·COME·BLOW·
ME·YOUR·HORN·THE·SHEEP'S·
IN·THE·MEADOW·

ROCK-A-BYE-BABY.

Rock-a-bye, baby, on the tree top,
When the wind blows the cradle will rock,
When the wind lulls, the cradle will fall,
Down will come baby and cradle and all.

DING-DONG-BELL

Ding-dong-bell,
Pussy's in the well!
Who put her in?
Little Tommy Lynn.
Who pulled her out?
Little Jack Sprout.
What a naughty boy was that
To drown a pretty pussy cat,
Who never did any harm
But killed the mice in his daddy's barn.

DING·DONG·BELL·PUSSY'S
IN·THE·WELL·WHO·PUT·HER
·IN?·

THERE·WAS·an·OLD·WOMAN·

There was an old woman who lived in a shoe,
She had so many children, she didn't know
   what to do.
She gave them some broth, without any bread,
And she whipped 'em all round and sent 'em to
   bed.

THREE WISE MEN OF GOTHAM

Three wise men of Gotham
Went to sea in a bowl,
If the bowl had been stronger
My story had been longer.

THREE·WISE·MEN·OF·GO-
THAM·WENT·TO·SEA·IN·
A·BOWL

THE·LITTLE·DANDY·

Oh when I was a boy and a pretty little boy,
With my little curly head of hair so sandy, O,
    All the damsels used to cry,
    What a funny rogue was I,
And they christened me the pretty little dandy,
      O.

But when I older grew, and something better
      knew
Than sucking lollipops and sugar-candy, O,
    Why, I was so spruce and gay,
    That the ladies used to say,
Oh! the pretty little fellow is a dandy, O.

Oh and then to end all strife I did get a little
      wife,
With a pretty little waist so handy, O.
    And a lazy boots am I,
    That she sings me lullaby,
Says I'm a good for nothing dandy, O.

RIDE·A·COCK·HORSE

Ride a cock horse
To Banbury Cross,
To see an old woman
Upon a grey horse,
With rings on her fingers and bells on her toes,
And she shall make music wherever she goes.

RIDE · A · COCK · HORSE · TO ·
BANBURY · CROSS ·

THE·PIGS·

'Do look at those pigs as they lie in the straw,'
  Said Dick to his father one day ;
'They keep eating longer than ever I saw,
  Oh, what greedy gluttons are they !'

'I see they are feasting,' his father replied,
  'They eat a great deal, I allow ;
But let us remember before we deride,
  'Tis the nature, my dear, of a sow.

'But when a great boy, such as you, my dear
    Dick,
  Does nothing but eat all the day ;
And keeps taking nice things till he makes him-
    self sick,
  What a glutton ! indeed, we may say.

'When plumcake and sugar for ever he picks,
  And sweetmeats and comfits and figs ;
Pray let him get rid of his own greedy tricks,
  And then he may laugh at the pigs.'

GOOD·NIGHT·&·GOOD·MORNING

A fair little girl sat under a tree
Sewing as long as her eyes could see;
She smoothed her work and folded it right,
And said, 'Dear work good night, good night.'

Such a number of rooks flew over her head
Crying 'Caw! Caw!' on their way to bed.
She said, as she watched their curious flight,
'Little black things, good night, good night.'

The horses neighed and the oxen lowed,
The sheep's 'bleat, bleat' came over the road,
All seeming to say, with a quiet delight,
'Dear little girl, good night, good night!'

She did not say to the sun Good night,
Though she saw him there like a ball of light,
For she knew he had God's time to keep,
All over the world and never could sleep.

The tall pink foxglove bowed his head,
The violet curtsied and went to bed,
And good little Lucy tied up her hair,
And said on her knees her evening prayer.

And while on the pillow she softly lay,
She knew nothing more till again it was day,
And all things said to the beautiful sun,
  'Good morning! Good morning! our work has
        begun.'

A·FAIR·LITTLE·GIRL·SAT·UN·
·DER·A·TREE·

LULLABY

Sleep, baby, sleep!
  Dad is not nigh.
Tossed on the deep,
  Lul-lul-a-by!
Moon shining bright.
  Dropping of dew.
Owls hoot all night,
  To-whit! to-whoo!

Sleep, baby, sleep!
  Dad is away,
Tossed on the deep,
  Looking for day.
In the hedge-row
  Glow-worms alight,
Rivulets flow
  All through the night.

Sleep, baby, sleep!
  Dad is afar,
Tossed on the deep,
  Watching a star.
Clock going —tick,
  Tack,—in the dark.
On the hearth—click!—
  Dies the last spark.

Sleep, baby, sleep!
  What! not a wink!
Dad on the deep,
  What will he think?
Baby dear, soon
  Daddy will come,
Bringing red shoon
  For baby at home.

MISTRESS·MARY

Mistress Mary,
Quite contrary,
How does your garden grow?
With cockle shells
And silver bells,
And marigolds all in a row.

MARY·MARY·QVITE·CONTRARY·
HOW·DOES·YOUR·GARDEN
GROW·

LITTLE·POLLY·FLINDERS

Little Polly Flinders
Sat among the cinders
Warming her pretty little toes.
Her mother came and caught her,
And scolded her little daughter
For spoiling her nice new clothes.

JACK·AND·JILL·

Jack and Jill went up the hill
   To fetch a pail of water,
Jack fell down and broke his crown,
   And Jill came tumbling after.

JACK·AND·JILL·WENT·UP
THE·HILL·TO·FETCH·A
PAIL·OF·WATER·

THERE·WAS·A·LITTLE·MAN

There was a little man,
   And he had a little gun,
And his bullets were made of lead, lead, lead.
   He went to the brook,
   And he saw a little duck,
And he shot it through the head, head, head.

He carried it home,
   To his good wife Joan,
And bid her make a fire for to bake, bake, bake,
   To roast the little duck
   He had shot in the brook,
And he'd go fetch her next the drake, drake,
    drake.

The drake was swimming
   With his curly tail,
The little man made it his mark, mark, mark,
   But he let off his gun,
   And he fired too soon,
So the drake flew away with a quack, quack,
    quack.

SONG·OF·SPRING

The country's now in all its pride,
   Now dressed in lovely green,
The earth with many colours dyed,
   Displays a lovely scene.
Ten thousand pretty flowers appear,
To deck the little children's hair,
     Fa-la-la-la, fa-la.

The cuckoo's picked up all the dirt,
   The trees are all in bloom.
If pleasant music may divert,
   Each bush affords a tune.
The pigeon sings in every grove,
And milkmaids warble songs of love.
     Fa-la-la-la, fa-la.

Come out into the cowslip-meads,
   The pleasant wood and spring,
And listen in the beeches' shades
   Where nightingale doth sing.
Sweet nightingale whose warbling throat,
Far, far excels my sorry note,
     Fa-la-la-la, fa-la.

THE·COUNTRY'S·NOW·IN·
ALL·ITS·PRIDE·

CHIT·CHAT·

Pretty little damsels, how they chat,
   Chit, chat, tittle-tattle.
All about their sweethearts and all that,
   Chit, chat, tittle-tattle-tat.
Up and down the City, how they walk,
And of the beaus and the fashions, how the damsels
    talk,
And now and then a little bit of slander is no balk
   To their chit, chat, tittle-tattle,
   Chit, chat, tittle-tattle-tat.

Pretty little damsels, go to cheapen in the shops,
   Chit, chat, tittle-tattle,
Pretty little bonnets, and pretty little caps,
   Chit, chat, tittle-tattle-tat.
A little bit of rouge, and a nice little fan,
A nice little picture of a nice little man,
Or any silly thing at all of which they can
   Chit, chat, tittle-tattle,
   Chit, chat, tittle-tattle-tat.

Pretty little damsels, how prettily they run,
   Chit, chat, tittle-tattle,
For a little bit of flattery, and a little bit of fun,
   Chit, chat, tittle-tattle-tat.
The pretty little nose, and the pretty little chin,
And the pretty little mouth, and the pretty little grin
And the nimble little tongue to keep others in,
   Chit, chat, tittle-tattle,
   Chit, chat, tittle-tattle-tat.

WINTER·SONG

When the trees are all bare, not a leaf to be seen,
And the meadows their beauty have lost ;
When nature's disrobed of her garment of green,
   And the streams are fast bound by the frost ;
When the shepherd stands idle and shivers with
      cold,
   As bleak the winds northerly blow ;
When the innocent flocks run for ease to the fold,
   With their fleeces besprinkled with snow.

In the yard when the cattle are foddered with
      straw,
   And they send forth their breath like a stream ;
And the neat-looking dairymaid sees she must
      thaw
   Flakes of ice that she finds in the cream.
Then the lads and the lasses in company join'd,
   Round the fireplace gather in glee,
Talk of fairies and witches that ride on the wind,
   And whistle and sing so do we.

WHEN·THE·TREES·ARE·ALL·
BARE·NOT·A·LEAF·TO·BE·SEEN

LITTLE·BO·PEEP·

Little Bo-peep has lost her sheep,
  And can't tell where to find them ;
Let them alone, and they'll come home,
  And bring their tails behind them.

Little Bo-peep fell fast asleep,
  And dreamt she heard them bleating ;
But when she woke, she found it a joke,
  For they were still a fleeting.

Then up she took her little crook,
  Determined for to find them ;
She found them indeed, but it made her heart
    bleed,
  For they'd left their tails behind them.

It happened one day, as she did stray
  Into a meadow hard by ;
There she espied their tails side by side,
  All hung on a bush to dry.

OLD·KING·COLE·

Old King Cole
Was a merry old soul,
And a merry old soul was he.
He called for his pipe,
And he called for his glass,
And he called for his fiddlers three.
Every fiddler, he had a fiddle,
And a very fine fiddle had he,
Twee tweedle-dee, tweedle-dee, went the fid-
     dlers.
   Oh, there's none so rare
   As can compare
With King Cole and his fiddlers three.

OLD · KING · COLE · WAS · A · MERRY · OLD · SOUL ·

LAST·NIGHT·THE·DOGS·DID·BARK·

Last night the dogs did bark,
 I went to the gate to see.
When every lass has got a spark,
 Will nobody come for me?
        And it's O dear! what will become of me?
            O dear! what shall I do?
            Nobody coming to marry me?
            Nobody coming to woo?

My father's a hedger and ditcher,
 My mother does nothing but spin,
And I am a pretty young lassie,
 Yet slowly the money comes in.
        And it's O dear! etc.

They say that I'm comely and fair,
 They say that I'm scornful and proud.
Alas! I must surely despair,
 For alack! I am getting quite ou'd
        And it's O dear! etc.

And now I must die an old maid,
 O dear! how shocking's the thought.
And alas! all my beauty must fade,
 But I'm sure it is none of my fau't
        And it's O dear! etc.

IS·JOHN·SMITH·WITHIN

Is John Smith within?
  Yes, that he is.
Can he set a shoe?
  Ay, marry, two,
Here a nail, there a nail,
  Tick tack too.

IS·JOHN·SMITH·WITHIN?
AY;·THAT·HE·IS·CAN·HE·
⌒ ⌒ ⌒ SET·A·SHOE? ⌒ ⌒ ⌒

JACK·SPRAT·

Jack Sprat could eat no fat,
His wife could eat no lean;
And so betwixt them both, you see,
They licked the platter clean.

HARK! HARK!

Hark! hark! the dogs do bark,
The beggars are coming to town,
Some in jags, and some in rags,
And others in velvet gowns.

HARK · HARK · THE · DOGS · DO
BARK · THE · BEGGARS · ARE · CO-
-MING · TO · TOWN ·

PRIMROSE·HILL·

As I was going up Primrose Hill,
  Primrose Hill was dirty,
There I met a pretty miss,
  And she dropped me a curtsey.

Little miss, pretty miss,
  Blessings light upon you.
If I had half-a-crown a day,
  I'd spend it all upon you.

GREY·GOOSE·AND·GANDER

Grey goose and gander, waft your wings together,
  gether,
And carry the good king's daughter over the
  one strand river.

GREY·GOOSE·AND·GANDER
WAFT·YOUR·WINGS·TOGETHER

TWINKLE·TWINKLE·

Twinkle, twinkle, little star,
How I wonder what you are,
Up above the world so high,
Like a diamond in the sky.

When the traveller in the dark
Thanks you for thy tiny spark,
He could not see which way to go,
If you did not twinkle so.

When the blazing sun is gone,
And he nothing shines upon,
Then appears thy tiny spark,
Twinkle, twinkle, in the dark.